my words

grant snider

HARPER
An Imprint of HarperCollins*Publishers*

To Anna, for all your wonderful words

My Words

For information address HarperCollins Children's Books, a division of HarperCollins Publishers, 195 Broadway, New York, NY 10007.
www.harpercollinschildrens.com

Library of Congress Control Number: 2019951210
ISBN 978-0-06-290780-6

The artist used pen and marker on paper and colored the illustrations digitally using Adobe Photoshop.
Typography by Chelsea C. Donaldson
20 21 22 23 24 RTLO 10 9 8 7 6 5 4 3 2 1
❖
First Edition

I love words.

Words can be

Words are ideas that break free and take flight.

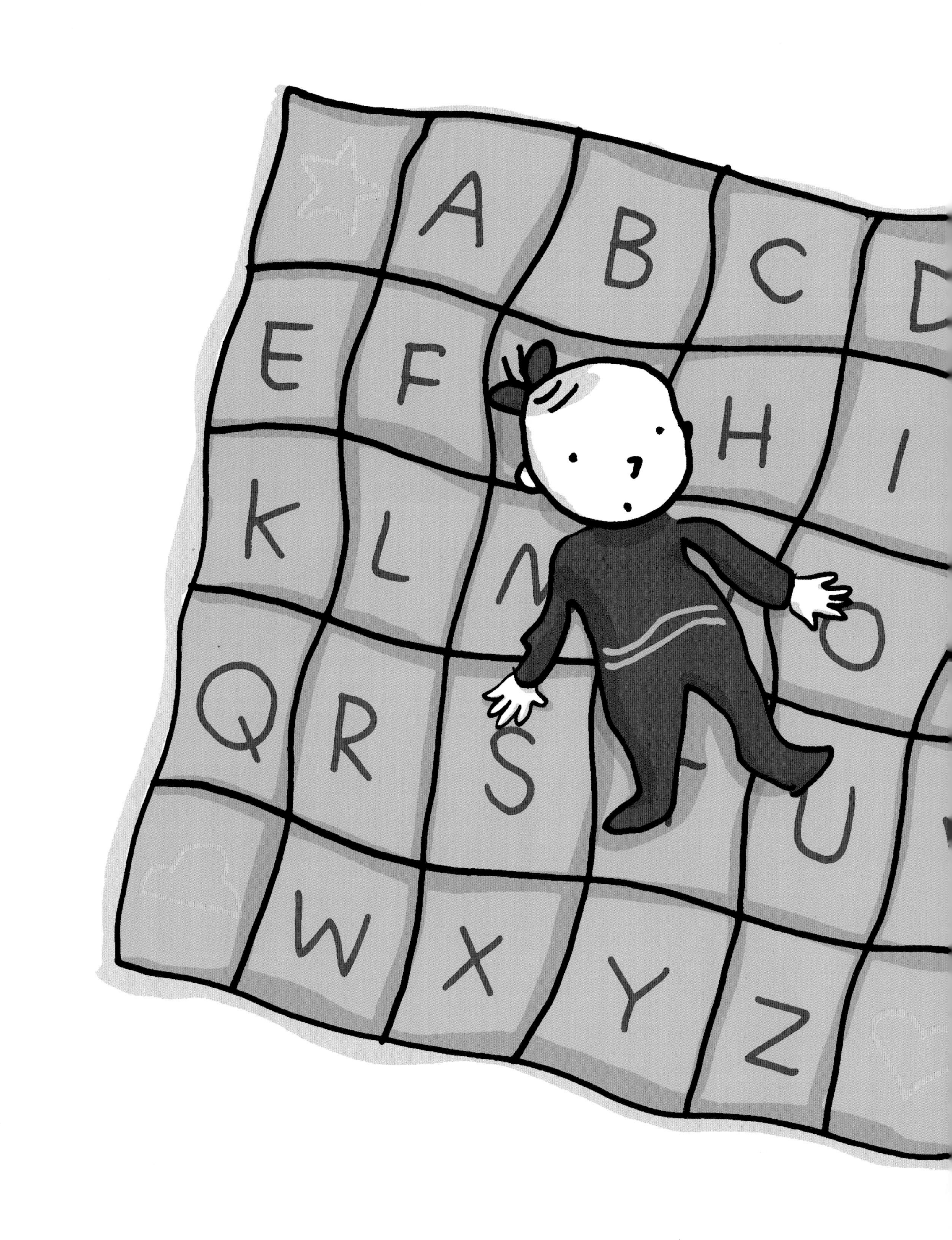
A B C D
E F H I
K L O
Q R S U
W X Y Z

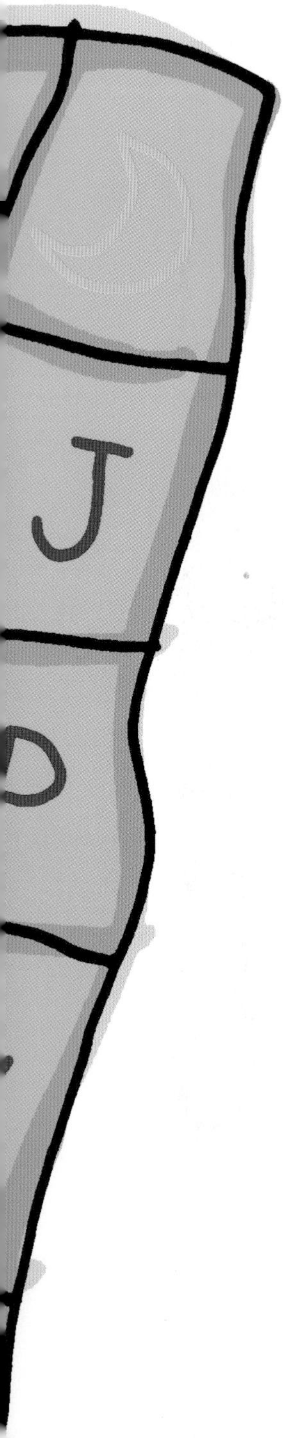

But I started with no words.

What was it like?

Waaa
oooh
eee
gaga

I had so much to say.

Waaa
oooh eee
gaga
yaaa

(And so did they!)

As I explored, I heard new words.

dog
no!

Then one day . . .

I said ball! (Simple and small.)

Then I said more:
ma!
da?

ba!

Sometimes my words
sounded very much alike:

guck.
guuck!

Some of them were right.

(Others, not quite.)

woof
woof

Pointing at things, I learned their names . . .

butterfly,

bumblebee,

bubble.
POP!

I found new words on rainy days . . .

splash!
squish
squish

. . . and talked to friends
in marvelous ways.
good morning, sun!
hi, robins!

hello, worms!
here, mom!

As I grew and grew, so did the mountain of words I knew.

bye
car
tree
and
up
dog
baby
eye
beep
kitty
uh-oh

Words are ideas that break free and take flight.
What will I do with my words?

I will use them to write!

I love words.